Pancakes for Breakfast

by Wendi J. Silvano

pictures by Susan Kathleen Harding

Richard C. Owen Publishers, Inc.
Katonah, New York

One morning, Grandma Rose
made our favorite breakfast -
pancakes!

We watched the stack
grow higher and higher
and higher.
Everyone was *so* hungry.

3

Grandma carried the stack
of pancakes to the table
very, very carefully.

The stack of pancakes
leaned to the left.

The stack of pancakes
leaned to the right.
We held our breath.

Then,
"a a a a h CHOO!"
Dad sneezed!

Grandma jumped!
Pancakes flew to the left.
Pancakes flew to the right.

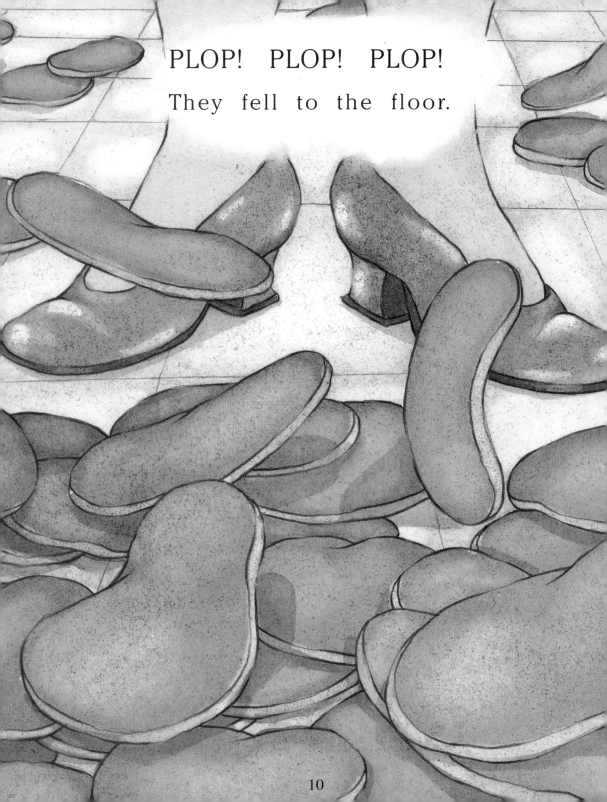

PLOP! PLOP! PLOP!
They fell to the floor.

Our dog Buster rushed in
and gobbled them all up!

That morning, we had cold, dry toast
for breakfast.